MR BROWN'S BAD DAY

To my lovely dad, who is my best
kind of Very Important Person xx – L.P.
For Kitt x – A.F.

First published 2020
by Nosy Crow Ltd,
The Crow's Nest,
14 Baden Place,
Crosby Row, London
SE1 1YW
www.nosycrow.com

ISBN 978 1 78800 397 1 (HB)
ISBN 978 1 78800 398 8 (PB)

Nosy Crow and associated
logos are trademarks and/or
registered trademarks of
Nosy Crow Ltd.

Text by Lou Peacock
Text copyright © Nosy Crow 2020
Illustrations © Alison Friend 2020

A CIP catalogue
record for this book
is available from the
British Library.

Printed in China.
Papers used by Nosy
Crow are made
from wood grown in
sustainable forests.

MR BROWN'S BAD DAY

LOU PEACOCK

Illustrated by
ALISON FRIEND

Mr Brown was a **Very Important Businessman.**
He always carried a **Very Important Briefcase**
and he worked in a **Very Important Office.**

He said things like, "Sell! Sell!"
Though sometimes he said, "Buy! Buy!"

People brought him **important** letters to sign
and there were lots and **lots** of meetings.

Mr Brown was **always** very, **very** busy.

But, no matter how busy he was, Mr Brown always went out for lunch.

Naturally, Mr Brown took his **Very Important Briefcase.**

It had **Very Important Things** in it, after all.

Today was Tuesday and so Mr Brown had tuna sandwiches.
He set the briefcase down and, as he ate his lunch,
he thought about the **Very Important Things**.

But, because Mr Brown was so busy thinking, he didn't spot the baby. He didn't spot the baby grab the handle of his **Very Important Briefcase**. And he didn't spot the baby take the **Very Important Briefcase** away.

Suddenly, Mr Brown realised the **Very Important Briefcase** was missing.

"My briefcase!" he said. "I must find it. It's full of **Very Important Things**."

Fortunately for Mr Brown, the baby
and the briefcase were not far away at all . . .

. . . but, **unfortunately** for Mr Brown,

the baby hooked the briefcase onto an ice cream cart . . .

and the ice cream seller pedalled away!

"Wait!" called Mr Brown. "Wait!
That's my **Very Important Briefcase!**"

Fortunately for Mr Brown, the ice cream
seller soon stopped . . .

. . . but, **unfortunately** for Mr Brown, some schoolchildren accidentally took the briefcase for a ride on the big wheel.

"Wait!" shouted Mr Brown. "Wait! That's my Very Important Briefcase!"

Fortunately for Mr Brown, the queue was moving quickly . . .

. . . but, **unfortunately** for Mr Brown,
when the schoolchildren got off the ride,
they took everything with them,
including Mr Brown's
Very Important Briefcase.

And then they went to catch the bus.

"WAIT!" bellowed Mr Brown. "WAIT!
That's my Very Important Briefcase!"

Mr Brown ran as fast as he could to the bus stop . . .

and was just in time to see the bus pull away.

Poor Mr Brown.

His hat had gone and his tie was wonky.
"This," said Mr Brown, "is a VERY BAD DAY."
But the Very Important Briefcase was full of
Very Important Things so . . .

. . . Mr Brown borrowed a tricycle . . .

even though it was a little too small.

past the tennis courts . . .

and around the lake . . .

He followed the bus **all** over town . . .

but he could never quite catch up.

When the children got off the bus, they took everything with them, including the **Very Important Briefcase.**

"Whose is this bag?" said the teacher.

"Not mine," said one child.

"Not mine," said another.

"Or mine," said a third.

"It's mine!"

gasped Mr Brown.

"Very Important Things inside!"

By now, it was dark and, because it was too late to go back
to the **Very Important Office**, Mr Brown went home.

When he got there, Mr Brown opened his **Very Important Briefcase** and checked that all the **Very Important Things** were still inside . . .

. . . his snuggly blanket,

his best book
of bedtime stories,

and his favourite teddy bear.

Then, with all the
Very Important Things
safe and sound,

Mr Brown settled down to the
Very Important Business of . . .

. . . bedtime.